Loggerhead turtles are an endangered species, and many organizations protect them.
However, one out of five thousand hatchings completes their journey to the Sargasso Sea.

While vacationing in North Carolina, we had the wonderful experience of witnessing a mother loggerhead turtle emerge from the surf and crawl onto the sand to lay her eggs. It was the most inspirational event to watch and led with a profound respect for this endangered species.

Even though Cletus, the Little Loggerhead Turtle, is an animated, funny children's story, the facts about loggerhead turtles are actual.

Cletus and Charley represent all the hatchings and their challenges journeying to the Sargasso Sea.

To change the world for the better, we must be kind, caring, and respectful to everyone.
 Always think with your heart, and you will never go wrong.

Remember how precious life is on earth, from humanity to the tiniest hatchling.   Be mindful of not polluting the planet, especially our oceans, where thousands of species and plant life exist.

Enjoy,

Lindalouise

Lindalouise

Lindalouise

Illustrations by

Kerrie Robertson

Cletus,
the Little Loggerhead Turtle

Charleston, SC
www.PalmettoPublishing.com

Cletus, the Little Loggerhead Turtle

Copyright © 2021 by Lindalouise

First Edition

Hardcover ISBN: 978-1-7345917-3-6
Paperback ISBN: 978-1-7345917-4-3
eBook ISBN: 978-1-7345917-5-0
LCCN #: TXu1-332-207

Dedication

***

Cletus, the Little Loggerhead Turtle, is dedicated to her family-husband, Bill,
three sons Billy, David, Tzyy, Mom, and the newest member, a grandson Cameron Wynn
and Bella Lynn, their furry family member.

Special thanks to Sophia and Mackenzie.

Special thanks to the wonderful volunteers who make the trenches
and safely guide the hatchlings to the ocean.

Special thanks to everyone at Palmetto for their guidance, support,
and professionalism in assisting authors.

One spring evening, a mother loggerhead turtle swam to the shore from the ocean when a full moon was shining brightly in the sky. She stopped in the surf, looked around, and crawled onto the beach using her front and back flippers. She needed to find a safe place to lay her eggs because many predators on the beach would disturb them.

Eventually, finding a sheltered place above the tide line, the mother loggerhead turtle began digging a large hole in the sand with her rear flippers. She laid a clutch of one hundred and twenty eggs. Then, she covered her eggs with sand, crawled back to the surf, and swam out to the sea. She would never return to that nest again. Her baby turtles would hatch one day, crawl toward the moonlight, and swim out to the sea as she did.

$\mathcal{I}$nside two of these leathery eggshells were two tiny turtles named Cletus and Charley.

They were brothers but opposite of each other. Cletus was a fun-loving turtle but very stubborn.

He always wanted to do things his way, even if it was not the best idea.

Eventually, tired Cletus was becoming very uncomfortable inside his shell and could not wait to leave it. Being inside his eggshell was annoying him, and the thought of freedom would be fantastic.

On the other hand, Charley was easygoing and usually went along with everyone else.

Unlike Cletus, though, Charley was quite comfortable and very happy inside his shell.

Seven weeks passed, and a full moon appeared over the ocean.

Eventually, Cletus and the other hatchlings were ready to crack open their shells using the single egg tooth in front of their noses.

Charley began cracking his eggshell and taking his time to do so.

Finally, after a few minutes, he looked over at Cletus and watched him open his shell with much excitement.

"Why are you in such a hurry?" asked Charley.

Cletus happily answered, "It is too cramped inside my shell. I am tired of being here and need to leave it at once!"

A few minutes later, Cletus happily broke his eggshell and emerged to the top of the nest, just like the other hatchlings.

Cletus was delighted being on top of the nest. He looked around and saw a full moon shining over the ocean. He saw strange birds flying above him and wondered about them. Cletus waited for his brother, Charley, and was overly excited for him to see everything too.

Not long after, Charley and a few hatchlings were the last ones surfacing to the top.

Their turtle shells were tiny in size, making them more likely to be eaten by seagulls or other predators.

All the other baby turtles began crawling instinctively toward the water. Cletus and Charley watched them. They could see ocean waves rolling back and forth in the distance, noticing that all turtles from their nest were heading that way.

"Look," pointed Charley, "the others are crawling in that direction. We should be following them!"

"No!" insisted Cletus. "Let us go the other way."

"You are very stubborn, Cletus," warned Charley, getting worried.

"We should climb this incline and get to the water before the others," insisted Cletus.

Cletus climbed the hill and reached the top. He noticed lights from houses in the distance and started crawling toward them.

"No," said Charley, "come back!"

Cletus turned around and slid down the hill.

"Wee! This is fun, Charley. Come and try this!"

"I do not think it is a good idea," answered Charley, "Let us follow the others."

"Race you to the water," laughed Cletus. "I am going my way."

Cletus began climbing the wall, and Charley started following the others.

Then, without delay, Charley called over to his brother, "Hurry Cletus, follow me! I will stay and swim near the shore until you catch up with me!"

Cletus watched Charley but wanted to continue going his way so he would reach the water faster than his brother.

Sitting on top of the hill was a tiny hermit crab, watching what Cletus and Charley were doing.

Then, graciously, he introduced himself to Cletus.

"My name is Leonardo," he said to Cletus. "Leonardo means strong as a lion. Look at these claws," and he held his pinchers proudly up for Cletus to see.

"I can see your claws are powerful!" Cletus told Leonardo.

Leonardo watched Cletus go up and slid down the slope several times.

"What are you doing?" questioned Leonardo.

"I don't know. I am trying to catch up with Charley!" answered Cletus.

"The other turtles are heading toward the water," said Leonardo.

"I just figured crawling along the top of this hill would be a shortcut to the water," explained Cletus.

"No, no," insisted Leonardo. "You are not listening to me! Stop climbing the hill and follow the others!"

However, stubborn Cletus did not listen. Instead, he climbed to the top of the hill and slipped back down!

Even though he thought sliding down the hill was fun, he was beginning to get tired and annoyed; his plan was not working at all!

Leonardo was frustrated that he could not convince his new friend to head toward the water like the others.

A little sandpiper named Oceana flew over to Leonardo and perched herself next to him. She had been flying around this beach for several years, watching the hatchlings emerging from their nest and swimming out to sea.

She introduced herself to Leonardo and Cletus.

"My name is Oceana, and it actually means ocean. I am a sandpiper, and I can fly amazingly fast!"

She moved her wings quickly up and down to show them.

"And look at my beautiful feathers," boasted Oceana, spreading her wings.

Cletus chuckled, "Yes, your feathers are beautiful, and your name is awesome too. I think it is cool that your name means ocean."

Leonardo agreed with Cletus and complimented her too.

"Maybe you can help me find my way to the surf so I can be with my brother?" pleaded Cletus.

"Why are you climbing and sliding down this hill?" questioned Oceana.

Cletus looked over at Oceana and insisted, "Climbing this hill and crawling along the top will help me reach the ocean waves faster than the others."

"Hey, while you are doing all this climbing, you better watch out for predators!" warned Oceana.

"What are predators?" inquired Cletus.

"Do you see the seagulls flying above?" warned Oceana. "They will swoop down and carry you away!"

"So, let them carry me away! The seagulls can give me a ride to the water," laughed Cletus.

"You are so silly," answered Oceana. "The seagulls only want you for dinner!"

"Squawk! Squawk!" Hearing the calls of the seagulls, Cletus noticed them flying above and became frightened. Leonardo was scared too. He did not want to show any fear of the seagulls in front of everyone. He remembered some awful experiences with them, especially when one picked him up and dropped him onto the sand.

Leonardo turned to Cletus and warned him, "Remember, there are other predators that wander on the beach, like foxes and raccoons. They are always searching for a turtle snack. You need to be careful!"

Cletus looked at his two friends for a moment and inquired, "Who made this trench?"

"This trench was made by people that volunteer their time protecting turtles like you. The sand walls are high so that you follow the light from the full moon and stay inside the trench until you reach the ocean. They hope you'll crawl directly into the surf, and nowhere else," explained Oceana.

"Now I understand why climbing this hill was difficult. I am supposed to go directly to the ocean's waves," moaned Cletus to his friends.

Looking at the ocean, Cletus realized his brother, Charley, and the other turtles had disappeared into the waves.

Now he knew climbing the walls of the trench was a bad idea!

Cletus felt frightened and alone because crawling toward the tide without his brother was something that terrified him. He missed Charley and wished he listened to him.

A hungry seagull spotted him, and Cletus did not notice it.

The seagull began flying downward toward him!

"Look out!" cried Oceana. "The seagull is coming, Cletus!"

We need to protect Cletus from the seagull," yelled Leonardo, holding up his pinchers toward the seagull.

However, as the seagull flew toward Leonardo, he crawled into the trench.

Oceana flew in front of Cletus and spread out her wings.

Leonardo managed to get under her wings too.

The seagull attempted to grab Cletus and Leonardo many times but missed.

They watched the seagull flying above them.

I hope this seagull gives up and flies away!" whispered Oceana.

"Me too," agreed Cletus.

"I second that motion," added Leonardo, pointing, and shaking his claw toward the seagull.

Oceana was concerned for the safety of her friends. She wondered if Cletus would ever make it to the ocean. However, she also worried about Leonardo. Even though he had strong pinchers to protect himself, a seagull can quickly grab Leonardo, too, because of his small size.

Oceana knew she needed to try and save her friends and fast.

The seagull finally disappeared!

It was quiet now; the three of them remained still in the trench and rested.

Cletus and his friends were exhausted from their ordeal.

Oceana knew she needed to help Cletus get to the ocean safely.

"We must get you to the surf for you to begin your journey to the Sargasso Sea," advised Oceana.

"Where is the Sargasso Sea located?" asked Cletus.

"The Sargasso Sea is in the North Atlantic Ocean with four currents surrounding it," explained Oceana.

"Are currents fish?" asked Cletus.

"No, no, currents are not fish. Currents are the way water flows in the ocean," clarified Leonardo.

"Then, what are the names of these currents?" questioned Cletus.

"Let me explain," responded Oceana. "To the west is the Gulf Stream. The Canary Current circulates on the east. At the top of this sea is the Northern Current. The Equatorial Current flows on the southern side. All four currents circulate in a clockwise motion, keeping tiny turtles and fish inside them."

"You will swim freely and safely within these four currents for about twelve years until becoming an adult," reassured Leonardo.

"Will I become large?" asked Cletus.

"Hold your horses, you ask a lot of questions," continued Oceana. "Your shell can grow about three feet in shell length, and you can weigh about two hundred and fifty pounds. Right now, you're only two inches long and weigh one ounce."

"Wow! I really will become exceptionally large!" laughed Cletus.

"Hold my horses?" laughed Cletus.

"Means wait," chuckled Oceana.

Leonardo added, "Inside the Sargasso Sea is a seaweed called Sargassum, where you will be able to hide from predators. There are plenty of algae, seagrass, jellyfish, clams, and mussels for you to eat. The currents of the Gulf Stream will help you get there. Your journey will take only three days!"

"It sounds like a wonderful place!" cheered Cletus.

Now, very excited, Cletus was looking forward to seeing Charley and the others.

Leonardo and Oceana began helping Cletus toward the surf when another seagull appeared and began circling them.

"I don't believe it," panicked Cletus. "Here comes another hungry seagull!"

Leonardo decided to crawl on top of the trench to distract the seagull. He was feeling very fearless and wanted to protect his friend. He held up his pinchers as the seagull came closer. Leonardo nipped the seagull, and it flew away!

The seagull flew down several times, attempting to grab Leonardo, and touched his head with its beak.

"Ouch, that hurts!" yelled Leonardo very loudly.

"Follow me!" said Oceana to Cletus.

She flew in front of Cletus, guiding him to the surf.

"It feels like I am crawling forever," agonized Cletus.

"Just hang in there," said Oceana.

She stayed in front of Cletus, guiding him to the water's edge.

The hungry seagull continued to circle them and flew downward several times, trying to grab Cletus.

At last, unsuccessful in its attempt, the seagull flew away!

Cletus was incredibly grateful.

41

Cletus made it to the surf, and warm ocean waves rolled over his little shell. He was happy to see his brother swimming next to him. Charley kept his promise and waited near the surf until Cletus caught up to him. The ocean waves began pushing them further and further out beyond the tide. Their tiny turtle shells were now floating in the warm water.

Cletus learned many life lessons from his friends—the two most apparent ones were the value of true friendship and how important it is to care for each other.

He learned to be brave through his friends' courageous efforts to protect him from many hungry seagulls.

Oceana and Leonardo shared knowledge about the Sargasso Sea and their experiences living on the beach with Cletus, which will prepare him for his latest adventure.

Cletus and Charley motioned goodbye with their tiny front flippers. They were safely on their way, and their journey was beginning.

During their travels, Cletus and Charley will meet more amazing friends. In addition, they will see and experience many incredible wonders from the ocean, like their mother and other loggerhead turtles have in the past.

About the Author

***

Lindalouise had imagined becoming an author of children's books since the age of nine. It had been a dream of hers and fulfilling that dream has been one of the most exciting adventures of her life.

She is a retired teacher who taught fourth grade for thirty years and found much joy in her rewarding career. The best part of the day for her was reading novels with her students and, of course, writing.

Lindalouise obtained a bachelor's degree and two master's degrees: one in Special Education and the other in Reading Specialization.

She currently resides in New Jersey with her husband, son, and a wonderful dog Bella. She also has two sons, who live in New York, and is immensely proud of her family and success.

Cletus, the Little Loggerhead Turtle, is inspired by her volunteering and guiding hatchlings to the water. Walking on the beach and witnessing a mother loggerhead turtle emerging from the surf and crawling onto the sand to lay her eggs is the most inspirational event to watch. It has left her with a profound respect for this endangered species.

CPSIA information can be obtained
at www.ICGtesting.com
Printed in the USA
LVHW071117240223
738938LV00007B/10